PARADISE HOUSE

The Echo in the CHIMNEY

HILARY McKAY

a division of Hodder Headline plc

Text Copyright © 1996 Hilary McKay
Inside Illustrations Copyright © 1996 Tony Kenyon

First published in Great Britain in 1996
by Victor Gollancz

The edition first published in 1998
by Hodder Children's Books

A Catalogue record for this book is
available from the British Library

ISBN 0 340 72288 6

Offset by Hewer Text Ltd, Edinburgh

Printed and bound in Great Britain by
Mackays of Chatham plc, Chatham

Hodder Children's Books
A Division of Hodder Headline plc
338 Euston Road
London NW1 3BH

Chapter One

There was a house in London called Paradise House. It was very old and very big. It had a square garden planted with rose bushes and surrounded by a hedge and a brick wall, three wide stone steps leading up to the front door, bats in the attic, beetles in the basement, and spiders throughout the whole building.

Long ago Paradise House had been the home of one rather rich family. Now it was divided up into flats and all sorts of people lived there instead. Among these people were Old McDonald the caretaker (who shared the basement with the beetles) and the three different families belonging to Danny, Nathan and Anna. Danny O'Brien, Nathan Amadi and Anna Lee were best friends. They were all nine years old and in the same class at school.

It was usually agreed that Nathan had more than his fair share of brains and that Anna was kinder than most people manage to be. Danny was famous for his love of animals. Any sort of animals; he was the type of person who could become fond of a beetle. This was not always easy for his friends and relations to live with, especially as he was also not very good at changing his mind. No matter what other people thought. This habit is known as stubbornness.

Danny and his mother lived in a flat at the top of Paradise House. It was a perfectly ordinary flat. It was not haunted.

It was not haunted and yet on the first night of the summer half term holiday Danny jerked upright in bed and knew that something unusual had woken him. He waited, staring into the dark, and it came again, a hoarse echoing shriek and then a whispering rustle. It was coming from the wall directly behind him. Danny felt his hair prickle and the skin on the back of his

neck become cold and tight. It was a long time before he realized that the tremendous thudding noise that seemed to fill the room was the sound of his own heart pounding.

For what felt like ages Danny sat motionless, too frightened to move or to call out, and then quite suddenly, like a light switching off, he fell asleep.

It was almost morning when he woke and heard the rustling again, but being able to see made Danny feel much braver. This time, instead of freezing with fright, he climbed out of bed and went to break the bad news to his mother that there was a ghost in his bedroom wall.

"Oh, for goodness' sake, Danny!" moaned his mother sleepily, "this is my first Saturday off work for weeks! You were only dreaming."

"I was wide awake," Danny told her earnestly.

"Well, you shouldn't have been wide awake," replied his mother. "Look at the time! Go back to bed! There's no such thing as ghosts."

"You wouldn't say that if you'd heard it screaming in the wall right behind me," said Danny.

"Ghosts don't scream *in* walls, they walk *through* them," murmured Danny's mother with her eyes tight shut.

"Swop beds!" pleaded Danny. "Perhaps then you'll hear it too."

"I don't want to hear it," protested his mother, yawning and yawning.

"Please," said Danny.

"Children!" exclaimed Danny's mother, suddenly lurching out of bed and grabbing her dressing gown. "Why ever did I have them? I must have been mad!"

"You only had me," pointed out Danny, climbing hastily into her bed before she could change her mind.

"More than enough," replied his mother grumpily. "Don't you DARE wake me up before eight o'clock!"

"*I* won't but IT might," said Danny.

"It won't if it knows what's good for it," replied his mother, shuffling crossly out of the room.

"Jolly brave," thought Danny, and wondered if ghosts were like dogs and only bothered people who they knew were frightened of them. He hoped this wasn't true and thought that if it was then it was most unfair. He grew warm and more comfortable and was just trying sleepily to decide whether he would be afraid of the ghost of a dog when, all at once, there was his mother quaking on the end of the bed.

"I told you so!" said Danny.

"What a terrible noise!" exclaimed his mother, too shaken even to notice this graceless remark. "I've never heard anything like it! Whatever can it be?"

"Ghosts," said Danny, very relieved to hear that he was not the only person being haunted.

"It couldn't possibly be," replied his mother, but Danny thought she sounded far from certain.

"What shall we do?" he asked.

"Do you think it could be mice?" asked his mother.

"No," said Danny.

"No, neither do I," agreed his mother uneasily. "As soon as it's properly light we'll go and find Old McDonald."

"I'm not surprised you're hearing things," said Old McDonald when they told him their story. "What with all the livestock that boy brings into the house there's bound to be something gets loose now and then."

"Nothing's got loose!" said Danny indignantly. "I haven't got anything *to* get loose!"   .

"Well then it's mice," answered Old McDonald, pouring himself another cup of tea. "No call to knock me up for mice, was there?"

"Were you in bed?" asked Danny.

"More or less," said Old McDonald, who had been up for ages but was never very helpful first thing in the morning.

"It isn't mice," Danny's mother said firmly. "I thought of mice myself. It's something much bigger than mice."

"Doubt if it was a rat," said Old McDonald. "There's never been rats in

Paradise House that I know of."

"Have there ever been ghosts?" asked Danny.

"Not on the second floor," said Old McDonald, as if to imply that the rest of the house was stuffed full of them.

"Please come and listen," begged Danny's mother. "I know it wasn't a ghost or rats or mice but it must have been something!"

"What sort of size?" asked Old McDonald, and Danny's mother said she thought it sounded about as big as a small sheep.

"A screaming sheep," added Danny, and Old McDonald at last began to be interested enough to follow them back upstairs to Danny's bedroom.

"Livestock!" he said immediately, catching sight of Oscar swimming round and round the goldfish bowl.

"It definitely wasn't Oscar," said Danny's mother.

"Well, it's all quiet here now anyway," said Old McDonald and he walked round the room slapping the walls with an enormous leathery hand to encourage the mice or rats or ghosts or sheep to come out and show themselves. After a few slaps on the wall above Danny's bed the horrible screeching suddenly began again.

"There!" said Danny's mother triumphantly.

"Ah!" said Old McDonald. "Right above the fireplace! It's the chimney making it echo so badly! I might have known!"

"Might have known what?" asked Danny, while his mother exclaimed, "But I didn't know there was a fireplace!"

"It's covered over," Old McDonald told her. "Plasterboarded up. They were all done years ago, but they're still there underneath. That'll be a bird."

Danny's mother groaned, and up in the chimney there was another dismal squawk, followed by a pattering sound.

"Bringing down soot," commented Old McDonald. "Poor creature."

Now that Danny knew it was a bird he could not think how he had imagined it to be anything else and he listened in growing

horror to the struggle in the chimney.

"It'll sort itself, given time," said Old McDonald.

"Sort itself?" asked Danny.

"One of those things," said Old McDonald.

"You mean it will die?" asked Danny bluntly, and Old McDonald did not reply.

"Perhaps now it's daytime it will see the light and fly back out," suggested Danny's mother hopefully.

"These old chimneys are all bends," said Old McDonald. "There won't be any light gets down to where it is."

"Can't we take down the wall?" pleaded Danny. "We must do something."

"You could open up the fireplace," said Old McDonald, after a moment's thought. "Give it a chance, anyway. It might come down."

Danny's mother groaned again and made signs to Old McDonald to shut up.

"Be a mucky job," said Old McDonald, taking no notice and speaking to Danny, "and no telling if it would work."

"It would ruin the wallpaper," protested Danny's mother, looking at the beautiful, expensive animal wallpaper she had bought and stuck up for Danny on his last birthday.

"Who cares about rotten wallpaper?" asked Danny, already tugging his bed from the wall.

"I do," his mother answered. "I'm sorry, Danny, but it will have to take its chance."

"It hasn't got a chance!" said Danny. "Please, Mum!"

Danny's mother looked helplessly at the wall, and then at Danny and Old McDonald.

"I can fetch up my tool box and have it clear in half an hour if you like," said Old McDonald.

The unhappy struggling noises came again. Danny's mother, knowing she really had no choice but to let Old McDonald go ahead, got Danny to move everything possible out of his bedroom before it became covered in soot. Old McDonald, suddenly helpful now he had got his own way, hurried downstairs for his tool box and a bundle of ancient paint-splattered sheets that decorators had once left behind. Danny helped his mother to spread them over the bed and chest of drawers and table and carpet while Old McDonald cut through the wallpaper and prised off the plasterboard. A sour, choking smell of soot filled the room as it was lifted away. In the darkness behind was a large sooty mound with shapes poking out of it.

"Leave this to me!" Old McDonald told Danny's mother, and she thankfully retreated to the kitchen. Danny could hardly bear to look himself. All the time Old McDonald had been working there had been no sound from the chimney.

"Do you think it's died already?" he asked, and glanced fearfully at the jutting shapes in the pile of fallen soot.

"More likely frightened with all the racket we've been making," replied Old McDonald as he shovelled the fireplace clear. "You're a one you are! Talking your mum into all this mess!"

"You helped," said Danny.

"She doesn't like mess, your mum," continued Old McDonald, ignoring him. "Nor birds in the house, for that matter. I remember her going into a panic when a sparrow got in. This'll be bigger than a sparrow."

"A pigeon?" asked Danny.

"More like a jackdaw," said Old McDonald. "They nest up in them old chimney pots. A young one might have strayed down."

There was more than just soot in the fireplace. They discovered sticks and pieces of brick and bones and feathers and, once, a whole dried, twisted ruin of a bird.

"There's worse things than ghosts," remarked Old McDonald when this appeared, and Danny agreed.

Eventually the fireplace was empty. Old McDonald straightened up and began to tie up the bag of soot and collect his tools together.

"Leave the brush and shovel," he told Danny when Danny went to pick them up. "You'll be needing them yet."

"Are you all finished?" called Danny's mother from the other side of the door. "Can I come in? Is it all over?"

"All but the waiting," replied Old McDonald.

They did not guess then how bad the waiting would be.

Chapter Two

Soot hung in the air like smoke. Already everything in the room was covered in a thin film of black dust. The smell in the air was so strong they could almost taste it.

"This is dreadful," said Danny's mother, coming in to inspect when Old McDonald had gone.

"It must be worse up the chimney," said Danny.

"I can't do anything about the chimney," replied his mother, rather crossly. "Go and have a shower, Danny, while I open some windows. You look grey!"

"Will you shout straight away if it comes out while I'm gone?" asked Danny.

"What!" said Danny's mother. "Does that mean I've got to wait in here?"

"Somebody will have to," Danny pointed

out. "It might come down at any time and it's bound to be frightened and flap about. And if it's quite big it will be much easier to catch it straight away before it gets loose in the room."

"Quite big? What do you mean 'quite big'?" asked his mother suspiciously.

"Old McDonald thinks it's a jackdaw," Danny explained.

"A jackdaw!" repeated his mother in horror. "One of those black things that live on the roof?"

"Yes," said Danny.

"But they're enormous!" moaned his mother. "Oh, Danny!" and she sank on to the bed and held her head in her hands. Until that moment she had thought of nothing larger than a sparrow or, at worst, a starling. It was not sensible to be so frightened, but she could not help it. Ever since she was a little girl she had been terrified of any bird caught in a house, and she would rather have faced a dozen ghosts than one panicking, flapping jackdaw. Even so, she knew that Danny was right and someone

ought to stay in the room.

"Have a very quick shower," she told him earnestly. "I don't know what I'd do if it came down while you were gone."

"Just try and hold on to it," said Danny.

"I couldn't possibly. I'm sure I would faint."

"I'll be as fast as I can," promised Danny.

Danny was very fast indeed, but before he returned the rustling and calling had begun again, and when he opened the door he found his mother crouched in the fireplace clutching a large bath towel (which she planned to throw over the intruder's head) and muttering desperately to herself.

"'And sang to a small guitar,'" Danny heard her say. "'O lovely Pussy! O Pussy, my love, What a'—Oh, Danny! Thank goodness you're back!"

"Why are you saying poems to it?" asked Danny, impressed by this thoughtful but unexpected behaviour.

"It keeps me calm," replied his mother, looking far from calm. "I always say poetry when I need to be calm. Haven't you noticed?"

"No," said Danny. "What poems do you say?"

"'The Owl and the Pussy Cat,'" replied his mother.

"What else?"

"Just 'The Owl and the Pussy Cat'," said his mother vaguely. "Now, Danny, I'm going to leave you to it. Shout if you need me. I'll be getting lunch."

For a while Danny sat in silence. The noise in the chimney started and stopped and started and stopped, and it occurred to Danny that the bird was not just trapped and frightened but also lost. In such total darkness it would have no idea which way it ought to go. It needed something to head for, so he knelt down at the fireplace and began to say, "It's all right. I'm down here. It's Danny. It's me. You'll be quite all right," very quietly, over and over again, and after a time it seemed to Danny that the bird was listening.

"Lunch," Danny's mother announced, popping her head round the door. "Are you coming out?"

"Couldn't you come in here?" asked Danny. "We could use my homework table if you brought another chair. It would be quite comfortable."

"I suppose I could," agreed his mother bravely.

It was not a very comfortable meal. Neither of them could take their eyes off the fireplace for more than a few seconds and Danny's mother jumped and dropped her fork at the slightest sound.

"Why do you just say 'The Owl and the Pussy Cat'?" Danny asked suddenly.

"It's the only one I know," she replied.

"Why didn't you learn another?"

"I didn't need to," she said. "'The Owl and the Pussy Cat' is enough. Danny, why do you think that bird hasn't come down?"

"Perhaps we're being too noisy," suggested Danny.

"I was thinking I ought to bring the vacuum cleaner in here," his mother told him, "but I suppose it won't be allowed."

"I'm sure the noise would frighten the bird," said Danny, "and the more frightened it is the longer it will take to come down. We mustn't use the radio or television either."

"No radio or television?" asked his mother.

"Or bang about in the kitchen or any awful loud singing," added Danny firmly.

"Thank you very much!" replied his mother, rather huffily. "In that case, I think I'll go shopping. We must eat, however many Trappist monks there are living up the chimney."

Soon after that she left for the shops, but not before she had looked back round the door and asked, "Anything I can get you?"

"Some crisps?" suggested Danny, guessing that this offer was his mother's way of making up for her crossness.

"Very noisy food, crisps," she replied. "I hope you intend to suck them! And what about putting in a little quiet dusting while I'm gone. I don't suppose that will offend His-Majesty-In-The-Dark!"

"Dusting?" asked Danny. "Me?"

"Why not?" asked his mother. "One day you'll have your own zoo, I suppose, and somebody will have to keep it dusted and it won't be me!"

"I don't believe in zoos any more," Danny told her. "I'm going to have my own animal hospital and safari park combined. I thought you could come and do the cooking."

"Oh, did you!" said his mother.

"It will probably be in Africa."

"Africa is very dusty indeed," his mother said firmly. "I've seen it on films. You'd better get practising."

"All right," agreed Danny.

For the next hour or so, Danny, in between looking up Trappist monks in the dictionary and spells of practice dusting, continued to chat reassuringly into the chimney and was rewarded by more flapping and more clouds of soot. The time passed very slowly. It was a great relief when there was a knock on the door and Anna bounced in to say that Old McDonald had told them the story of the trapped bird, and Nathan had promptly purloined a clothes prop and two feather dusters and invented a jackdaw-extractor.

"He's in an awful hurry to use it," continued Anna, busy with a length of washing-line at the bars of Danny's window. "He said to tell you to come down straight away while there's nobody about to fuss—"

"How does it work?" interrupted Danny.

"From the roof," Anna replied cheerfully. "It will take all three of us though; one to climb up and one to hold the stepladder and one to pass up the jackdaw-extractor and keep a look out. Come on!" And before Danny had time to protest she had rushed him out of the flat and downstairs into the garden where Nathan was struggling to erect Old McDonald's stepladder on top of his mother's kitchen table.

"I can't be long," said Danny, "in case it comes down while I'm out here."

Nathan said that it wouldn't take long, and explained that it was simply a matter of climbing on to the table and up the stepladder and via the washing-line to Danny's second-floor window, from where (with the aid of the bars) it would be an easy task to reach the guttering and then the roof.

"Then," said Nathan triumphantly, "all you have to do is hop up to the chimney and poke down the hole with my brilliant jackdaw-extractor, and there you are!"

"Stuck on the roof," said Danny.

"The big danger," continued Nathan, ignoring him, "is if someone comes back suddenly and starts making a fuss—"

"I would have thought the big danger would be falling off the roof," remarked Danny.

"Stacks of washing-line for safety ropes," said Nathan cheerfully.

"Strong as strong," added Anna. "We swung on it to check."

"Well, I suppose it's better than doing nothing," admitted Danny.

Old McDonald discovered them just at the critical moment when Danny was beginning the washing-line ascent to the window-sill, so that was the end of that idea. Luckily he was not the sort of person to tell tales.

"But what *will* you do?" asked Anna, when she visited Danny later that day. "What if it's not down by night?"

"It's got to be down by night," said Danny's mother.

"Will Danny still sleep in here if it isn't?" asked Anna, looking at Danny's bed which was stripped down to the bare mattress and covered with a dust sheet.

"Of course I will," replied Danny.

"You can't, Danny," said his mother. "I'm not having your quilt and bed covered in soot and, anyway, you wouldn't stay in here last night. You were frightened; you know you were."

"It's different now I know what it is," replied Danny. "And I've dusted loads of soot away. It's nearly all gone."

"I don't care," said his mother. "That quilt is brand new and I shall have to get the curtains cleaned as it is. Enough is enough!"

"Wait!" said Anna suddenly, and hurried out of the room. A few minutes later she was back again, her arms full of sleeping bag.

"You can borrow this," she told Danny triumphantly.

"Oh no, he can't!" said Danny's mother.

"Whatever would your mother say?"

"I asked her before I brought it up," replied Anna. "She said I could. And, anyway, it's mine. I got it for my birthday."

"Thank you," said Danny.

"And she said, 'Good luck, Danny', and Dad said to let him know if you need any

help when it comes down. Even if it's in the middle of the night."

"It *must* be down before then!" said Danny's mother despairingly. But it wasn't.

Anna's sleeping bag was very comfortable but Danny slept badly that night. Every rustle from the chimney jerked him back into wakefulness again, and then, so that the bird would not think itself completely deserted, he would climb out of bed to whisper, "It's all right, it's me, it's Danny. Come down. It will be all right . . ."

"This is terrible," said his mother, coming in with hot chocolate at two o'clock in the morning.

"Sorry," replied Danny.

"It's not your fault," replied his mother, hugging him. "You're doing your best."

On Sunday the bird was still alive.

"Two nights!" said Danny. "Poor bird, poor bird."

They gave up quietness and tried noise

instead. They shone lights up the chimney and banged on the wall. By this time everyone in Paradise House knew what was happening and they visited Danny as if he was a patient in hospital. Anna's father popped in on his way to work, and in the afternoon Old McDonald stomped all the way up from the basement to hear the latest news.

"What about a chimney sweep?" Danny's mother asked him.

"They use vacuum cleaners these days," said Old McDonald. "I doubt it would do any good, even supposing you could get one to come out."

"It's just like when we were waiting for Chloe to be born," remarked Nathan when it was his turn to visit. "Everybody wondering."

"I've got a book where the children who live in an old house climb around in the chimneys to explore," Anna remarked.

"Don't you dare start trying to climb that chimney!" said Danny's mother, so crossly that the bird in the chimney was startled and croaked.

"It sounds terrible!" said Anna, nearly in tears, and Danny exclaimed, "I don't see why we can't just knock the beastly wall down!"

"I don't think I can stand another night of this," Danny's mother told the two old Miss Kent sisters when they arrived a few minutes later. They brought chocolates and a jigsaw for Danny, making it seem even more like hospital visiting.

"You're tired out," said the oldest Miss Kent. "Why don't you come and sleep downstairs tonight and one of us will stay with Danny?"

Danny's mother hugged her but said she couldn't possibly. "I wouldn't sleep, anyway," she added. "This really can't go on much longer!"

All the same, it did go on. It went on for another night.

Chapter Three

On Monday morning Danny's mother said, "Old McDonald has an idea."

Danny, who had spent another night of dozing and waking and whispering to the bird in the chimney, looked up dopily from Anna's sleeping bag.

"He thinks we should light a fire," continued his mother.

"NO!" shouted Danny, stumbling to his feet.

"Listen!" said his mother. "Not a hot fire. A smoky fire made with something damp. Smoke might make it drowsy enough to let go of whatever it's clinging on to and tumble down."

"Might it really?"

"It's worth a try," said his mother.

"All right," said Danny, and later he

allowed Old McDonald to light a small fire of sticks and then smother it with grass cuttings as soon as it began to burn. Thick, choking smoke poured up at once. For a moment nothing seemed to be happening and then there was a huge shower of soot and dreadful, terrified squawking.

"Put it out! Put it out!" screamed Danny, and tears poured down his cheeks as Old McDonald, realizing he was doing more harm than good, raked the fireplace clear and put the fire out.

"Don't cry, Danny," begged his mother.

"I'm not!" said Danny furiously. "It's the smoke. Go away! Leave me alone! It's the smoke, I tell you!"

Just at this inconvenient moment Nathan entered the room.

"I've had *another* brilliant idea!" he announced. "I've been listening to the jackdaws on the roof . . . What's the matter? Why is Danny . . . ?"

"Smoke in his eyes," replied Old McDonald, glaring at Nathan.

"Oh but," said Nathan, "I thought . . .

43

Anyway, listen! I've been looking at the jackdaws on the roof outside. They're calling to each other, two big ones and two littler ones with shorter tails, and I'm sure the big ones are teaching the little ones to fly. Every time the big ones call, the little ones come flying a bit further. Come and see, Danny! If you could copy a jackdaw noise perhaps it would work with yours and you could call it down."

"Chawk!" called the jackdaws on the roof.

"It's a dead easy sound to copy," said Nathan. "'Chawk!' Like that!"

"Yes," said Danny, listening carefully. "But they make it longer. 'Chaawk! Chaawk!' And then that sort of clicking sound. Like this."

"Do it again!" ordered Nathan, shielding his eyes against the sun to stare up at the roof, and when Danny did it again he said, "I saw them look down at you."

"Honest?" asked Danny.

"Honest," said Nathan. "Do it again and watch."

Danny did it again and this time he saw for himself how the jackdaws on the roof cocked their heads to look.

"Come on!" he said. "It might work! Quick!"

It took a long time. It took hours and hours. Eventually Nathan was forced to go home for his dinner but Danny stayed, alternately calling the jackdaw call and saying, "Come on! It's Danny! It's Danny! Listen!"

The bird was definitely listening. Old McDonald and Danny's mother saw that at last something was really working and hovered in the doorway, afraid to interrupt. The rustling echoes came closer and closer. Soot billowed from the chimney in clouds. There was a sudden tumble of rubble and then an open wing flashed out and a moment later Danny held the bird in his hands. It lay quite still and hardly struggled.

Old McDonald, with Danny's mother following, came hurrying into the room.

"Oh, Danny!" exclaimed his mother in horror when she saw the quivering bundle of blackness that Danny was holding.

No one could have guessed it was a jackdaw. It hardly looked like a bird at all. Its wings were nothing more than mangled bunches of feathers and it gasped for air as if it was drowning. Worst of all, where its eyes should have been were two enormous balls of soot.

"Better give it to me," said Old McDonald, when he saw those dreadful eyes.

"No!" said Danny.

"Danny," said his mother gently, "it might be kinder . . . "

"It wouldn't be kinder," said Danny, hurrying away to the bathroom before they could make any more of these frightful suggestions.

"What are you going to do?" called his mother.

"Wash it," said Danny.

In the bathroom he turned on the cold tap of the hand basin and gently moved the

jackdaw's head into the stream of water. The jackdaw sneezed and drew back for a moment and then, of its own accord, put its head back under the tap. It seemed as if it

understood exactly what to do. It did not panic at the strange world it had suddenly dropped into, nor at the clutch of Danny's hot hands, nor at the feel of running water, which it could never have known before. It opened its beak to drink and bathed its head. Jet black water began to stream down the plughole. It was such a lovely sight to see the soot being washed away that at first Danny didn't notice what had happened to the jackdaw's eyes until suddenly it turned its head and looked at him. It looked straight at him, as clearly and carefully as one person looks at another, and Danny saw that its eyes were clear silver. Clear, clean, silver, shining as bright as rain.

"Hallo, Silver," whispered Danny. "It's me, Danny. It's Danny. It's all right now."

It was quite plain that Silver knew Danny. He already knew Danny's voice that had stayed with him for so long and guided him out of the dark, and now he knew Danny's face, and the pattern of Danny's eyes and mouth and shaggy brown hair was fixed in the jackdaw's memory.

The water running from Silver changed from jet black to very dark grey. Silver began to shiver and Danny decided that was enough washing for one day. The nearest thing handy to wrap Silver in happened to be his pyjama jacket, still lying on the bathroom floor. Danny had to let go of Silver for a moment when he bent to pick it up but the bird did not try to escape. Even when he was swathed in blue and purple dinosaurs he did not struggle. Danny

carried him through to the living room and Silver sat quietly on his lap while Old McDonald closed up the bedroom fireplace and Danny's mother opened all the windows and dusted and vacuumed.

"He's not frightened at all," said Danny, and thought how lovely it would be to have a jackdaw as a friend, riding on his shoulder like a parrot and flying down to his hand from the sky.

"Silver," said Danny softly, and the jackdaw's eyes, which had been half closed with weariness, suddenly opened.

"It's all right," said Danny. "It's Danny," and Silver relaxed again.

"He's tame as tame," said Danny to his mother, when Old McDonald had gone and she came to see the visitor, but he was wrong. It seemed that Silver was only tame with Danny. Danny's mother's face and voice meant nothing to him at all. He saw a huge advancing stranger and went into a panic. The room filled with squawks and shrieks and not all of them came from the jackdaw. By the time Danny managed to get Silver safely into his bedroom, his mother was pale and shaking and Silver himself was exhausted. Danny wrapped him up again and stowed him in the corner of a large box, left a bowl of bread soaked in water within reach, switched out the light, so that Silver was left in half darkness, and went off to find his mother.

"Are you cross?" he asked anxiously.

"Of course I'm not," she replied. "It's a wild bird and it went wild, that's all. What have you done with it?"

"I took the Lego out of my Lego box and put him in there."

"Did you shut the lid?"

"No, but I'm sure he's safe. He looked really tired; he was sort of swaying. I think he nearly fainted."

"*I* nearly fainted," said his mother.

"You'll get used to each other," said Danny comfortingly.

Danny's mother did not reply at once. She was remembering the time that Danny had made a zoo in the attic (with disastrous results to the roof). Danny was sometimes not very sensible when it came to animals.

"What would you like to happen to your jackdaw?" she asked him. "If you could have anything."

"Like a wish?" asked Danny.

"Yes, like a wish. What would you wish for?"

"I'd wish he could fly away," said Danny immediately, and Danny's mother sighed with relief.

"Like a proper wild bird?" she asked.

"Yes, like a proper wild bird," agreed Danny. "But still knowing me, so he would fly down to meet me when he saw me outside. It would be brilliant if he would come to the school playground sometimes, or the park. Think what a surprise people would get when they saw him!"

"Well," said his mother, "the first thing to do is to get him flying. Perhaps he can already."

"He must be old enough," said Danny. "He must be the same age as the ones on the roof that me and Nathan were watching. They could fly."

"He'll never learn to use his wings in a Lego box," said Danny's mother. "I suppose it means he'll have to stay loose in your bedroom for a day or two, and you'll have to stay with him, and I can't say I like the idea, but I can't think of anything else we could possibly do."

"He might not be strong enough to fly," pointed out Danny. "Not after three days in the chimney with nothing to eat."

"We will feed him up," said Danny's mother firmly.

When Danny peered cautiously into the box before he went to bed he saw that Silver had already begun the feeding up. The bowl of bread and water was completely empty

and Silver was hunched in a corner, fast asleep and still wearing Danny's pyjama jacket. There were little black triangles all around the bowl where Silver's sooty chin had rubbed on the rim.

"I wish I could have seen him eating it," thought Danny drowsily, and fell asleep himself.

Chapter Four

The next morning, Danny's mother cooked scrambled eggs on toast for breakfast, one plateful for Danny and one for Silver.

"Scrambled eggs are strengthening," she remarked to Danny.

She was rather proud of the way he had worked so patiently to get Silver out of the chimney and she had made up her mind not to complain about the awful inconvenience of having him in Danny's bedroom. All the same, she couldn't get used to the idea of a jackdaw living in the house, and thought the sooner he was strong enough to take care of himself the better it would be.

"How is he now?" she asked Danny when he brought the empty plates back into the kitchen.

"Much better, thank you," Danny told

her happily. "He loved the eggs!"

"What is he doing?"

"Standing on the table tidying up his feathers. He's just had a bath in his water bowl."

"Perhaps he's getting ready to fly," said Danny's mother hopefully.

"I still don't know if he *can* fly," replied Danny. "His wing feathers are all broken and raggedy where he must have knocked them in the chimney."

"He can flap," said Danny's mother, "so I don't see why he can't fly. What's the difference?"

"I bet there's loads of difference," said Danny seriously. "Like paddling and swimming. Swimming's much harder. You don't want him to fly away already, do you? He's only just come!"

"Only just come!" repeated Danny's mother. "It feels like he's been here for months!"

"Don't you like him?"

"I would like him much more outside where he belongs," replied Danny's mother, nobly not mentioning the mess in Danny's bedroom, her own private horror of flapping wings and the constant trail of soot that Danny had begun to leave everywhere he went. "And I can't help thinking it's an awful waste of your holidays."

"But I'm having a lovely holiday *now*," exclaimed Danny, sounding so astonished that his mother could not help laughing.

A little later on Anna's father arrived with a book for Danny.

"I suddenly remembered this," he said. "I don't quite know what you'll make of it; it wasn't really written for children, but there's a big section in it about jackdaws. I used to read it myself when I was a boy. How is the invalid getting on?"

"Fine, thank you," replied Danny. "He's had scrambled eggs and toast, and a bath in a bowl of water, and he's not a bit scared when he's on his own with me. I think he knows me."

"Of course he does," replied Anna's father.

"I wish he'd make friends with other

people as well, though," said Danny. "It would be much easier to look after him if he was more tame. Mum wouldn't mind him so much, and Anna and Nathan could come and see me."

"Getting lonely shut in that bedroom all day?" asked Anna's father.

"I'd only like to show him to people," said Danny.

"Well, it probably won't be for much longer," said Anna's father. "And don't forget, once you turn him loose he will have a much better chance on his own if he hasn't learnt to trust humans too much."

"I know," said Danny.

"Jackdaws need jackdaws," Anna's father told him. "I must get off to work! Good luck, Danny! Try and get him flying."

Back in Danny's bedroom Silver was standing at one end of the table half asleep after his enormous breakfast. All around the bowl Danny had filled for him to bathe in was a large circle of sooty splashes. Danny sat down opposite and looked at Anna's father's book. It was called *King*

Solomon's Ring, a title that meant nothing at all to Danny who had never heard the legend of King Solomon and the magic ring that allowed him to understand the language of animals. To help Danny, Anna's father had put markers in the chapters where jackdaws were described. Danny

turned to these places first and very soon forgot the puzzling title. It was the most fascinating book he had ever read and had obviously been written by someone who understood jackdaws. As Danny read on he realized that Anna's father had been right when he said that jackdaws needed jackdaws. It seemed that older jackdaws not only taught the young ones to fly, but also jackdaw language and skills, what was safe and what was dangerous, as well as where to feed and roost and play.

For Danny the morning passed quickly, as he alternately daydreamed aloud about owning his own wild tame jackdaw and read out useful advice to Silver. Silver listened earnestly to the daydreams and hopped solemnly across the table to inspect the pictures, and Danny would have been perfectly happy if he had not known that he ought to be outside copying real jackdaws instead of looking up his relations in books.

"I don't *want* you to fly away," Danny told him. "But you've got to. You'd better start learning after lunch."

At first learning to fly was dreadful. Danny, with the best of intentions, began completely the wrong way round. It did not occur to him that if Silver's parents had been teaching him the lesson would have begun with something solid to take off from, such as the roof of Paradise House, and ended up in the air. Instead Silver's lesson began in the air and ended up with

something solid. Danny climbed on to a chair and, with a vague memory of kite-flying in the back of his mind, launched Silver upwards towards the ceiling. For a moment Silver was too surprised to do anything at all, and when he did begin to flap, the flapping did not help him. There was quite a loud thud, which was Silver colliding with the opposite wall, followed by a very loud thud, which was Danny crashing to the floor from his chair in his hurry to reach him.

"Whatever is it?" asked Danny's mother, rushing into the bedroom when she heard the noise.

"I've killed him! I've killed him!" wailed Danny, scooping up Silver and hugging him to his chest. "I threw him into the air to teach him to fly and he crashed and now—"

"He's not dead!" interrupted his mother. "His eyes are open and he's looking around. Stop squeezing him and see for yourself!"

She was right. Silver, although frightened, was quite unhurt. Danny's mother stepped hastily towards the door as he

began to flap and struggle to be free.

"Put him in his box until he calms down," she advised Danny. "I expect all baby birds have a few bumps! Come away and leave him alone for a while. It seems as if I've hardly seen you since Saturday! I've been making caramel shortbread and it should be cool enough to eat by now. Leave that bird in peace and go and wash your hands while I cut it up."

Caramel shortbread was a holiday treat that Danny had almost forgotten, and by the time he had finished his third piece he was feeling a lot happier.

"Do you think Silver would like some?" he asked.

"No!" replied his mother. "I've spent half my holidays worrying about that bird and I've turned over my son and his bedroom to him and I've cooked and cleaned and whispered and stayed up all night but I am NOT wasting caramel shortbread on a jackdaw! And that's that! Besides, he's been eating all day. He'll get so fat he'll never fly."

"He didn't act as if he would ever fly this afternoon," remarked Danny.

"You did it all wrong," said his mother. "You couldn't swim if you'd never seen water until someone dropped you into the sea from the top of a cliff! You ought to do it in stages. Couldn't you put his food on the floor next time you feed him and leave him on the table. I'm sure he'd soon learn to use his wings if he had to flap down to it. And then, when he's managed that, put his food on the table and him on the floor and see how he gets on the other way round."

This sounded so sensible that as soon as Silver had recovered from his crash-landing Danny put it into practice. It worked perfectly. By the end of the evening Silver could get himself from the table to the floor and back again as if he had been doing it for weeks. At first he did it to reach the grated cheese that Danny held out to him, but by bedtime he was doing it for fun.

"I never thought you'd learn so quickly," Danny told the bird, half proud and half

sorry because his time with Silver seemed to be passing so quickly.

Silver, who was on the floor taking his fifth bath of the day, shook his ragged wings and fluttered up to join Danny, who had returned to his book. Danny had been worried after the first disastrous flying lesson that Silver would be afraid of him, but Silver was not. He hopped right up to where Danny was sitting and looked straight into his face.

"You can fly," said Danny. "I think I'll have to let you go tomorrow." And before he could stop them, two large tears had splashed down on to *King Solomon's Ring*.

Chapter Five

"It's raining!" thought Danny in his dreams and woke up. It was very early morning. Bright sunlight shone through the gap in the curtains and outside he could hear the chatter of jackdaws on the roof. Even before Danny opened his eyes he could feel that he was being watched, but when he looked Silver was nowhere in sight. It wasn't until there was a pleased cluck of satisfaction from above Danny's head that he saw the bird perched on the curtain rails, drying his feathers after an early morning bath. The drops of water from Silver's wings must have been the rain of Danny's dreams.

Danny was still admiring him when his mother poked her head cautiously round the door.

"Hallo!" she said. "It's a beautiful sunny

morning . . . Goodness! Look where that bird's got to!"

"Yes," said Danny proudly, and suddenly he made up his mind to let Silver go at once, straight away, while it was still a bright morning and there were jackdaws about that he could follow.

"I'm sure you're right," agreed his mother when he told her. "I wouldn't say it to get rid of him, but it's really time he went."

"After he's had some breakfast but before there's people about," said Danny, and five minutes later Silver was eating scrambled eggs and corned beef at Danny's homework table while Danny pulled his clothes on and his mother hurried around Paradise House asking people to stay indoors for a little while longer.

"He's going to miss him if he goes," she remarked to Anna's father. "He has more to say to that bird than he does to most people; and I'm sure he's been reading aloud to him from that book of yours!"

"Good for Danny," said Anna's father.

"I thought he'd like it."

"I'm afraid it's getting rather sooty," Danny's mother told him.

"Honourable soot," said Anna's father.

Upstairs in Danny's bedroom there was a feeling of urgency. Danny, having decided that Silver must go, could not bear to linger over goodbyes, and Silver seemed equally impatient, never settling in one place for more than a few moments.

"Come on, then," said Danny, seizing a chance while Silver was close by and picking him up. Quite suddenly it seemed that there was nothing more to say to Silver, and nothing more to do except let him go.

They reached the garden just at the moment when the jackdaws were circling around the roof before setting off on their morning flight for the park where they spent their days.

"Oh!" exclaimed Danny in disappointment. "We're too late!"

Even as he spoke Silver seemed to leap from his hands. He flew clumsily, heaving his tattered wings through the air, but he made it to the garden wall. There he landed and called and called to the disappearing jackdaws, and to Danny's absolute amazement his call was answered. One of the birds that had left the roof seemed to stop in mid-air and turn back towards him. A moment later Silver had an adult jackdaw beside him, and seconds after that another arrived. Danny felt as if he might explode with excitement. These birds must be Silver's parents, and after nearly five days they had remembered and come back for him. Danny had never even hoped for such a miracle.

The adult birds were coaxing Silver to fly with them. Again and again they took it in turns to leave the wall and head off in the direction of the park. Silver glanced doubtfully down at Danny as if to see what he thought of this ambitious plan.

"Go on, Silver!" urged Danny, and Silver gathered his courage and left the wall. This time he had someone to follow, and, as Danny watched, the adult birds guided him

higher and higher. Then they turned, and carefully, one each side of him, led him slowly out of sight.

Paradise House exploded into cheers. From every window people waved and called. Danny's mother came running down the steps, caught Danny and hugged him. Nathan and Anna, still in their pyjamas, came jumping down after her. The Miss Kent sisters mopped their eyes and told Old McDonald they had never been so pleased and Old McDonald blew his nose and replied that they were a pair of old ninnies.

This unkind remark scattered the last of the magic. Nathan and Anna were caught by their mothers and dragged inside to get dressed. Nathan's baby sister, Chloe, who was not used to being ignored for so long, began to howl and was carried indoors. Danny's mother disappeared and so did Old McDonald. Soon there were only Danny and Anna's father left staring up into the blue.

"Well," said Anna's father. "Good work, Danny. That's one more bird in the sky."

That morning Danny thought he had seen the last of Silver but he had not. Jackdaws live for years and their memories are excellent. Long after Silver's tattered wings had grown sleek and whole and *King Solomon's Ring* had been read and re-read from cover to cover, a jackdaw came down from the sky and visited Danny. Every now and then, in the garden or in the park, there would be a swoop and a pause and a glance of recognition from two clear silver eyes.

"Very nice," remarked Anna's father, who happened to be present on one of these happy days, "to have a jackdaw for a friend."

"Very nice," said Danny, watching as Silver disappeared into the bright sky. "Just what I wanted."